IF I COULD DRIVE AN
AMBULANCE!

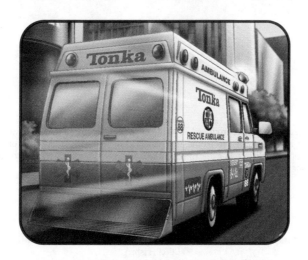

by Michael Teitelbaum
Cover Illustrated by Tom LaPadula
Interiors illustrated by Isidre Mones and Marc Mones

SCHOLASTIC INC.
New York   Toronto   London   Auckland   Sydney
Mexico City   New Delhi   Hong Kong   Buenos Aires

For EMT workers past, present, and future—heroes all.
Special thanks to Peter Auricchio for giving freely of his time and expertise.

ISBN 0-439-43433-5

HASBRO and its logo and TONKA are trademarks of Hasbro and are used with permission.
© 2003 Hasbro.
All Rights Reserved. Published by Scholastic Inc.
SCHOLASTIC and associated logos are trademarks and/or registered trademarks of Scholastic Inc.

Library of Congress Cataloging-in-Publication Data Available

10 9 8 7 6 5 4 3   03 04 05 06 07

Printed in the U.S.A.
First printing, January 2003

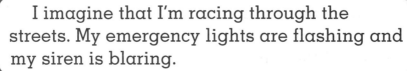

What if I could drive an ambulance?

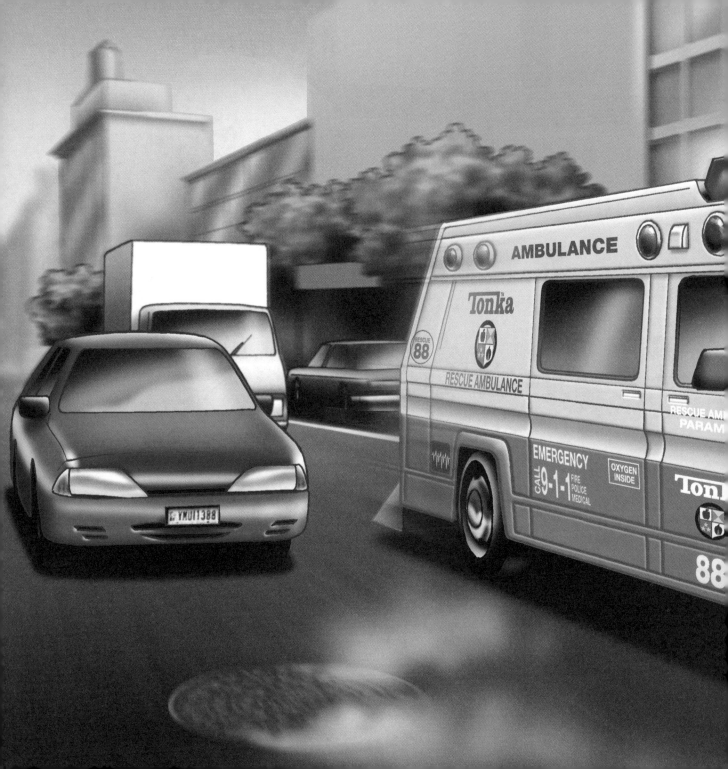

Every ambulance has two people. My partner is named Dina. We are both trained emergency medical technicians. We're called EMTs for short.

Someone has called 911 to report an emergency. A dispatcher — the person who got that call — contacts the ambulance driver closest to the emergency.
That's me!

I have to be careful to slow down at red lights and stop signs.

The ambulance dashboard has switches to control the lights and siren.

I also have a computer that provides me with information. It tells me about the injured woman, and it gives directions so that I can reach her quickly.

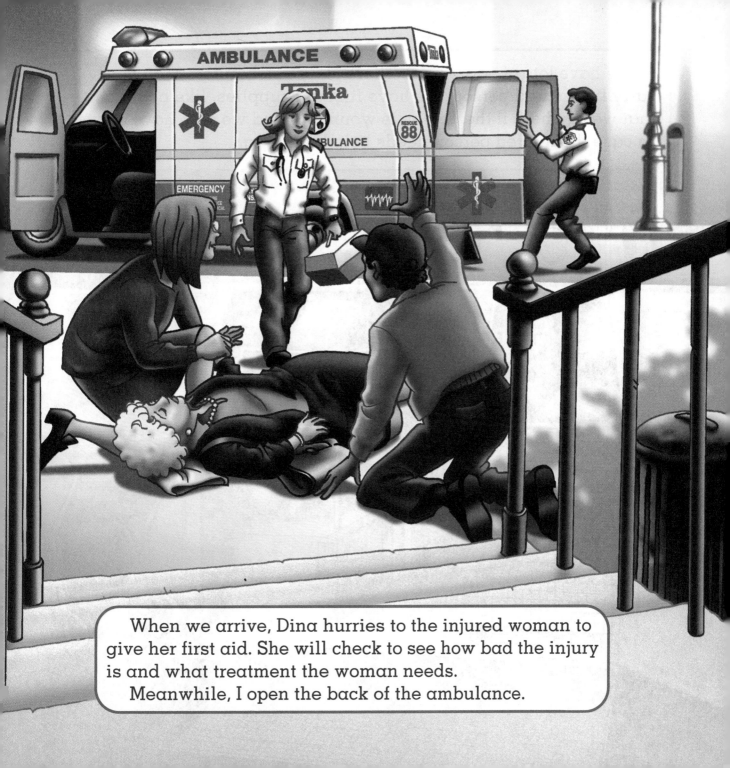

When we arrive, Dina hurries to the injured woman to give her first aid. She will check to see how bad the injury is and what treatment the woman needs.

Meanwhile, I open the back of the ambulance.

We have lots of equipment. There is a stretcher here that we use to carry the injured person. We have first aid supplies, like bandages, so that we can help if the person is wounded. And we also have oxygen in case the injured person needs help breathing.

Dina tells me that the woman has broken her leg. We pull out a stretcher.

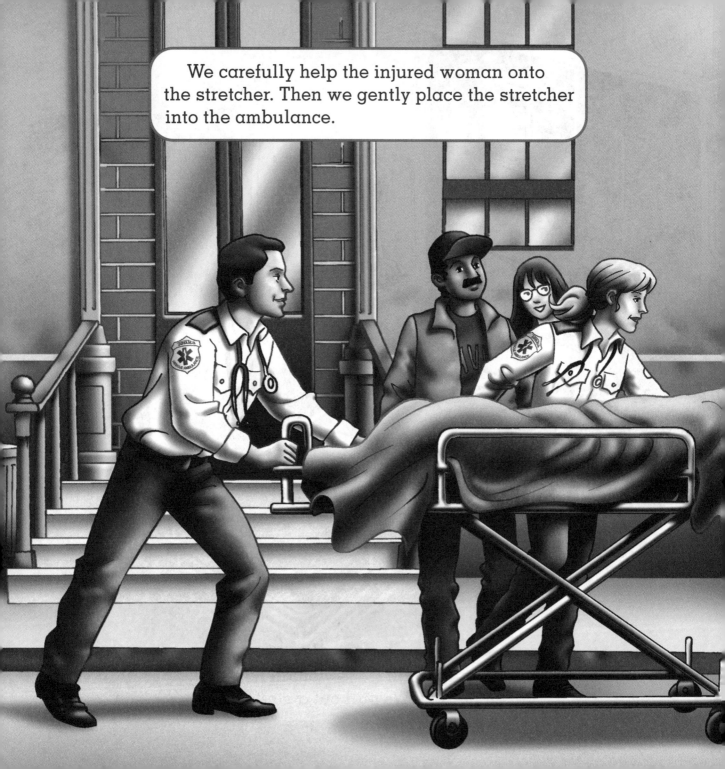

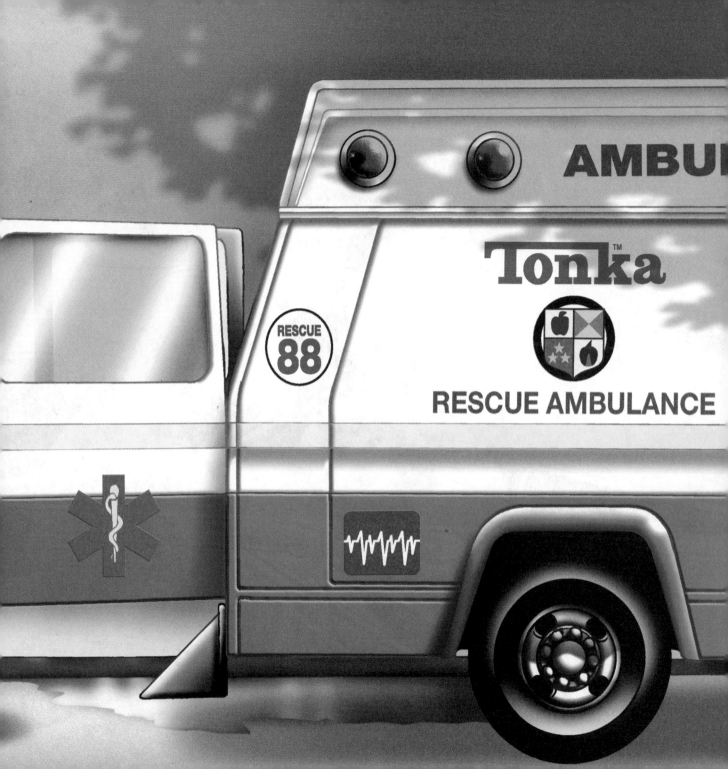

At the hospital, doctors and nurses take over.
They'll take good care of the injured woman.

I would help lots of people if I could drive an ambulance!